Einstein

Isambard

Willow

Bun

To Carolyn, who loves red squirrels

First published in the UK in 2019 by Usborne Publishing Ltd., Usborne House, 83-85 Saffron Hill, London EC1N 8RT, England. www.usborne.com

Text copyright © Diana Kimpton, 2019

The right of Diana Kimpton to be identified as the author of this work has been asserted by her in accordance with the Copyright, Designs and Patents Act, 1988.

Illustration copyright © Usborne Publishing Ltd., 2019

Illustrations by Sofia Cardoso.

The name Usborne and the devices ♀⊕ are Trade Marks of Usborne Publishing Ltd.

A CIP catalogue record for this book is available from the British Library.

JFMAM JASOND/19 05257/1 ISBN 9781474960250 Printed in the UK.

CHAPTER 1

"Come quickly," barked Hilton as he raced into the kitchen of the Primrose Tea Room.

"Why?" asked Amy Wild. She wasn't surprised to hear the small dog talking. The magic necklace she wore around her neck gave her the power to understand animals.

"Isambard says someone needs help,"

replied Hilton. "He has called a clan meeting."

"That's enough, Hilton," said Mum, as she lifted a batch of cakes out of the oven. "Amy can't come now however much you bark. She's promised to help us with the baking."

Hilton's ears drooped, and he gave a gentle whine.

"Oh! Look at that," said Mum. "It's almost as if he understands what I'm saying."

Amy was tempted to tell her mum that he did, but she knew she mustn't. Her magic power had to stay secret so that no one could misuse it.

Her great-aunt stepped over to the table and looked at the mixture Amy

was whisking. "That looks as if it's ready," she said. Then she added in a whisper only Amy could hear, "Is it important?"

Amy nodded and sighed with relief. It was good to know that Granty had guessed what her problem was. She had been the keeper of the necklace before she gave it to Amy, and she was the only other human in the world who knew that it was magic. Mum didn't, so she would need a little more persuading.

"Please can I go?" Amy begged.

"I don't know," said Mum. "We've still got all the icing to do."

"I'm sure that doesn't need three of us," said Granty. "You and I can manage by ourselves while Amy takes Hilton out." Then she winked at Amy, without letting Mum see.

"I suppose that's all right," said Mum reluctantly. "But don't be late for tea."

"I won't," said Amy. She dumped her whisk in the sink, rinsed her hands under the tap and followed Hilton to the back door.

Granty's parrot, Plato, was already there, waiting for them. Like Amy and Hilton, he was part of the Clamerkin Clan — a group who tried to help all the other animals on the Island of Clamerkin.

They raced down the garden together until they reached the clump of bushes at the far end. Hilton and Plato slipped easily between the branches, but Amy was bigger so she had to push her way through to reach the clearing that was the clan's almost-secret hideout.

The four cats that made up the rest of the clan were already there. Willow, the Siamese, was sharpening her claws on a tree trunk. Einstein, the Persian cat from the school, was washing his fluffy white fur, while the grubby tabby cat called Isambard was gazing longingly at a plane flying high overhead. In the middle of the clearing lay the fat black cat from the baker's shop. His name was Bun and, as usual, he was doing nothing at all.

Sitting beside him was a squirrel who Amy had never met before.

"Wow! Look at that bird!" said the squirrel, as he stared at Plato. "Those colours don't look natural. What's the matter, mate? Did you fall in a pot of paint?"

Plato fluffed out his feathers in annoyance. "I'll have you know that I am a parrot, and these colours are exactly how a proper parrot should look."

"Oh, la-di-da," said the squirrel. "I didn't realize we had such a posh bird in our midst." He pointed at his chestnut fur and added, "Now me – I'm a red squirrel. And this is what I call a natural shade of red."

Plato opened his mouth to reply, but Amy was quicker. "Is it you who has the problem?" she asked, in an attempt to change the subject.

"Me and all my friends," said the squirrel. "They call me Casper, by the way."

"Hello, Casper," chorused the four cats, Hilton and Amy together. Plato didn't join in. He stuck his beak in the air and refused to say anything at all.

Casper didn't seem to notice. "We live in the oak tree at the top of Home Meadow," he said. "That's me and the other squirrels and the woodpeckers and the owl and the nuthatch and both the wrens and the robins and the blue tits and a big family of chaffinches and several long-eared bats and—"

"Okay," said Einstein. "I think we've

got the message."

"And we all know the tree," said Amy. "It's so big and beautiful and such a brilliant place to play."

"It's good for climbing too," said Isambard.

"So what's the problem?" asked Amy.

"It's the men," said Casper. "They came to look at the tree this morning, and I heard them say they're going to cut it down."

Hilton's mouth dropped open in horror. "They can't do that."

"Yes, they can," said Willow. "People have been talking about it all afternoon in the post office. Everyone is very upset."

"So are we," said Casper. "We'll all lose our homes. So I've been sent here to ask the clan to stop them."

"How can we do that?" asked Hilton. He stared at Amy as if he expected her to know. But she didn't.

There was a long pause. Amy chewed her thumbnail while she struggled to think of an idea. Hilton and Plato both scratched their heads, and all four cats licked their paws thoughtfully.

Suddenly Plato tapped his beak on a branch to summon their attention. He waited until they were all listening, and then he announced, "We'll have a campaign. I've seen lots of them on TV and they're often about saving trees."

"What exactly is a campaign?"
asked Bun. Then he added hopefully,
"Can you eat it?"

"No, you can't," explained the
parrot. "A campaign is marching up
and down and carrying placards and
chanting 'Save our tree'." His voice rose
higher and higher as he spoke, and

he was hopping from foot to foot in
excitement.

Hilton looked doubtful. "I suppose
that might be fun."

"But it wouldn't work," said Willow.
"Only Amy would understand what we
were chanting."

"And we can't carry placards because we haven't any hands," said Isambard.

"Speak for yourself," said Casper.

He picked up a pebble with his front paws and threw it at the tabby cat.

"That's not very nice," said Isambard, jumping out of the way just in time.

"He's not," said Plato.

"So placards and chanting are out," said Einstein. "What else does campaigning involve?"

Plato plumped out his chest

proudly. "We can chain ourselves to the tree. That always seems to work."

"I'm not doing that," said Bun. "I wouldn't be able to go home for tea."

"That might do you good," said Casper. "You wouldn't be so fat if you ate less."

The black cat hung his head miserably until Hilton came to his defence. "I agree with Bun. I don't like the idea of chains either."

"Neither do I," said Amy.

"It would be pointless anyway," said Isambard, who lived with the local mechanic and knew masses about machinery. "The men would just cut through the chains with bolt cutters." He paused and added wistfully,

"Wonderful things, bolt cutters."

"So how are we going to save the tree?" asked Einstein.

There was another long pause. Then Amy said, "I think all of you are right."

"So the parrot really is a silly colour," said Casper.

"Correction," said Amy. "I think all of you except the squirrel are right. Plato's right about needing a campaign, and the rest of you are right about us not being able to run one."

Bun looked puzzled. "So what are we going to do?"

"We're going to get the humans on the Island to do the campaigning for us."

CHAPTER 2

When Amy got back to the kitchen,
she found Mum, Dad and Granty
sitting at the kitchen table. They were
deep in conversation, but they looked
up when Amy sat down in her place.

"We were just talking about the oak
tree," said Mum, as she handed Amy
a plate of egg salad. "The one in Home
Meadow."

"I loved that tree when I was a boy," said Dad. "I always played there when I came to Clamerkin for my holidays."

"And you weren't the only one," said Granty. "Generations of Clamerkin children have played around that tree. It's over a hundred years old."

"I wish they weren't going to cut it down," said Amy, without thinking.

Mum's eyes opened wide with surprise. "How did you find out about that? We only just heard about it ourselves."

"Careful," Hilton growled from his basket.

Amy didn't need the warning. Her mind was already racing to think of a reply that wouldn't give away her secret power. "A friend told me," she said at last. "She heard about it in the post office." It wasn't a lie, but it wasn't the complete truth either.

"That's how we know too," said Dad. "Everyone was talking about it when I went to buy some stamps."

Amy breathed a silent sigh of relief and concentrated on balancing a knob of butter on top of her potatoes. So far, so good. Now everyone knew about the tree, maybe they would start campaigning without her having to do anything else.

Then Granty sighed and said, "I'll really miss that tree."

"So will I," said Dad.

"And me," said Mum. "Home Meadow won't be the same without it."

Amy looked at them in amazement. "Aren't you going to do something to save it?"

"Like what?" asked Granty.

"Like have a campaign – with marching and chanting and placards

24

saying *Save our tree*."

Dad reached over and patted her hand. "I admire your enthusiasm, Amy, but it's not *our* tree. It belongs to Mr Townsend. He's just bought Heron House and all the land that goes with it, including Home Meadow. So the tree belongs to him, and he can cut it down if he wants to."

"So we need to make him not want to," said Amy. "And it will be easier to campaign now we know where he lives. We can march up and down in front of Heron House and wave placards at him whenever he goes outside."

"No we can't," said Mum. "It would make him cross, and then he might change his mind about letting everyone

on the Island go on using Home
Meadow."

"That's right," said Dad. "We don't
want to lose the field as well as the
tree."

"And we don't want to start an
argument with someone who's only
just moved here," added Granty.
"Clamerkin is a friendly place to live,
and we want it to stay that way – tree
or no tree."

Amy could tell there was no point
in arguing. They had already made
up their minds. But she couldn't
give up now – that would mean
letting down Casper and all the other
creatures who had asked the clan
for help. There must be some way to

change Mr Townsend's mind without
making him cross.

Amy thought about the tree problem
all night. She even dreamed about
crowds of birds and animals pleading
with her for help. But she had no ideas
in her head when she woke up, and she
still hadn't worked out a solution by
the time she had to leave for school.

Einstein trotted up to her as she
stepped through
the school gate.
His fluffy white
tail was stuck
straight up in the
air, and his face
was full of hope.

"When are they starting the campaign?" he asked.

"Never," said Amy. Then she told him everything her family had said last night.

As he listened, Einstein's tail drooped lower and lower and so did his ears. By the time she had finished, he looked totally miserable. "I don't like that squirrel much, but I don't want him to lose his home."

"Neither do I," said Amy. "There must be something we can do. We just need to work out what it is."

At that moment, the school bell rang and Amy ran to follow the rest of the juniors inside. The classroom was loud with the buzz of conversation. Everyone was talking about the oak tree and its fate.

"Isn't it dreadful?" said Amy's best friend, Veronica, as they sat down next to each other. "I love that tree."

"But you can't climb to the top," sneered Nathan Ballad from the desk behind them. "I'm the only one who has ever done that."

"No, you're not," said Amy. "Tom's done it too."

"So have Jade and Josie," said Veronica.

Nathan stuck his nose in the air and looked superior. "But neither of *you* have. So I'm still better than you two wimps."

"He's as annoying as that squirrel," mewed Einstein, who was sitting beside Amy's chair.

Before Amy had a chance to reply, Mrs Damson, their teacher, clapped her hands for attention. She was standing at the front of the room and beside her stood a boy Amy had never seen before. His hair was dark and curly, and his eyes were wide with fright. He was clutching his school bag in front of him like a shield.

"This is David Townsend," Mrs Damson announced. "He's just moved into Heron House with his parents so he's going to join our class."

"Townsend," said Jade.

"Heron House," said Josie.

"Your dad's going to cut down our tree," said Tom.

David gulped and tightened his grip

on his bag. "It's not my fault," he said
in a very quiet voice.

Amy felt sorry for him. It wasn't
so long ago that she'd been the new
student standing in front of the class,

and she still remembered how scared she had been. It must be awful for David to get such a bad response from everyone. If only there was something she could do to help.

CHAPTER 3

"This morning we're going to continue with our study of the environment," announced Mrs Damson when the class had settled down. "Last week we looked at the beach, so now we're going to study Home Meadow."

"It's a good thing we're doing it now," said Nathan. He glowered at David and added, "It won't be the same when his dad has cut the oak tree down."

"There's no need to be unpleasant, Nathan," said Mrs Damson. "David's already explained that it's not his fault." She clapped her hands for attention. "Now get into pairs so I can share out the tasks."

There was a brief scrabble while everyone organized themselves. Jade paired up with Josie, as usual, and Amy chose to work with Veronica. No one picked David and no one picked Nathan. The two

boys stood on opposite sides of the
room, eyeing each other suspiciously.

Nathan stuck his nose in the air,
crossed his arms
and turned his back
on David. "I'm not
working with him,"
he declared.

David tried hard
to look as if he didn't
care. But he failed.
He looked around
the room anxiously,
like a cat surrounded
by a pack of angry
dogs.

That reminded
Amy of how alone

she'd felt when she first came to the school. No one had wanted to be her friend either. "We could split up," she whispered to Veronica. "Then one of us could work with David."

"You do it," her friend replied. "I'm almost as cross with his dad as Nathan is, and I'd be sure to let it show."

So Amy walked over to David and smiled. "Would you like to work with me?" she asked.

A look of relief flooded David's face. "That would be brilliant." He glanced over to Nathan and added, "I don't think he likes me."

"He doesn't like anybody much," said Amy. "Except himself, that is." Then she realized that Einstein was right. Nathan was just like that annoying squirrel, and she grinned as she imagined him with tufts on his ears and a big bushy tail.

Mrs Damson handed them both a clipboard. "Your task is to study the oak tree and make a list of all the wildlife that you find there."

Then she gave Nathan and Veronica two hoops. "I want you to lay these on the grass and count how many different plants you can see inside them."

"That's a wimpy job," said Nathan. "I want to do the oak tree study."

"You would have done if you'd agreed to work with David," said Mrs Damson with a smile. "I'd already decided he would have that task."

"Huh!" grumbled Nathan. He stomped out of the building and set off towards Home Meadow, swinging his hoop violently from side to side, while Mrs Damson and the rest of the class followed at a safe distance.

As they walked, Amy asked David the question that had been bothering her ever since Casper had explained his problem. "Why does your dad want to cut down the tree? It's not doing anyone any harm."

"He says it spoils the view," said David.

"But it's a beautiful tree," said Amy. "Surely it makes the view better."

"Dad says it stops him seeing the sea

properly, and it's completely useless so there's no point in keeping it."

Amy was horrified. "It's not useless. It's home to lots of birds and animals and insects. You'll see in a minute." As she spoke, she was filled with hope. If she could show David how important the tree was, he might be able to help her save it.

When they reached Home Meadow, the juniors scattered in all directions to carry out the tasks they had been given. Amy and David were the only ones who had to go to the oak tree. But when they reached it, there wasn't a living creature in sight – not even a solitary bee. There were no sounds and no movement. The leaves hung

motionless in the warm, still air and
so did the rope swing tied to one of the
branches.

"It looks like you were wrong," said
David.

"No I wasn't," said Amy.
She looked up into
the tree and
raised her
voice to
make
sure all
its residents
could hear
her. "I'm
sure you'll be
able to persuade
your dad to keep the

tree when you've seen how many birds and animals live in it." She crossed her fingers, hoping that at least some of them would take the hint.

Then she turned to David and whispered, "We need to sit down and keep very, very quiet."

"You weren't very quiet just now. In fact, you were shouting."

"I know," said Amy, as she struggled to come up with an explanation. Then she gave up, shrugged her shoulders and added, "Silly me."

They sat down in the shade with their clipboards on their laps and their eyes fixed on the tree. At first, nothing happened. Then some of the leaves rustled.

David leaned forward eagerly. "Maybe there is something there," he said softly.

"Stay still and quiet," whispered Amy. "Wild creatures are easily frightened by unexpected movements and noises."

For a moment, she saw eyes peering out from the mass of green. Then

Nathan's hoop hit the tree with an enormous thump, and they all disappeared.

"What do you think you're doing?" she yelled at Nathan. There was no point being quiet now.

"Trying to hook this hoop over that branch," he yelled back. He grabbed hold of the rope swing and launched himself into the air. "Anything's better than counting stupid plants."

"Nathan Ballad," called Mrs Damson in her sternest voice.

"Come here at once. It's not playtime yet."

To Amy's relief, Nathan picked up his hoop and slunk away. With any luck, their teacher would keep him busy so he couldn't wreck her plans again.

"Has he frightened everything away?" asked David. "Or maybe there wasn't anything to frighten in the first place."

"Oh there was," said Amy. "And there still is. Didn't you see the eyes?"

David stared at her in disbelief. "Eyes? What eyes?"

"So you didn't. That's a pity." She gazed up into the tree and said, "Let's try again," in a loud voice. Then she

turned to David and whispered, "We
need to be very quiet."

"You're doing it again," said David.
"Shouting at the tree and then telling
me to be quiet."

"Silly me," said Amy again, wishing
she could think of a sensible excuse.

They sat down in the same place
as before and waited and waited and
waited. Amy could feel her panic
rising. Maybe none of the creatures in
the tree were going to show themselves.
Then something hard hit her on the
nose.

CHAPTER 4

"Ouch!" said Amy, as the bang on her nose was rapidly followed by something equally hard hitting her ear.

"Ow!" said David, rubbing his forehead where he'd been hit too. "What's happening?"

"I don't know," said Amy. As she spoke, something hit the top of her head and bounced off – but this time she managed to catch it. "It's an acorn," she said, holding it out to David.

"I don't understand," he said as two more acorns hit him – one on each ear. "We've been sitting here for ages without anything happening. Why have acorns started falling down now?"

A chuckle from the leaves above made Amy look up. Casper was sitting on a branch holding an acorn in each front paw. As soon as he realized she was watching, he threw one at Amy and one at David.

Amy ducked just in time. David wasn't so lucky. The acorn hit him hard on his nose. "I don't like this tree,"

he said, as he put his clipboard on top
of his head for protection.

Amy did the same with hers. Then
she pointed at Casper. "It's not the tree
doing it. It's that squirrel."

Casper scampered along the branch,
picked up two more acorns and threw
them hard. But this time they didn't
hit Amy and David. Instead they

bounced harmlessly off the clipboards.

"You're spoiling my fun," the squirrel grumbled. He picked up another acorn and looked at the two humans as if he was deciding which one to throw it at.

"Stop that at once!" yelled Amy.

Casper shrugged and dropped the acorn harmlessly to the ground. "There's no point in carrying on if I can't hit you anyway," he said. Then he bounded away, leaping from branch to branch.

"That's amazing," said David, who didn't realize the squirrel had been talking. "It's almost as if he understood what you were saying."

"I'm sure he didn't," said Amy quickly. "He was just scared by me making so much noise."

Just then, Mrs Damson blew her whistle to attract everyone's attention. "Time to finish," she announced. "We'll go back to the classroom so I can look at your results before lunch."

"Ours aren't very impressive," said David.

Amy wrote *red squirrel* on her clipboard in large letters and underlined it three times to try to fill up the available space. "At least we saw something," she said.

"I wish we hadn't," said David, as he wrote *nasty squirrel* on his board. "If that's the sort of animal that lives in this tree, I'm really glad my dad is cutting it down."

The hope Amy had felt earlier

disappeared like a popped balloon.
There was no chance of David
persuading his dad to change his mind
now. She felt absolutely miserable as
she trudged back to school with the
rest of the class. How could Casper
have been so stupid? It was such a good
plan, and he'd ruined it.

"What's wrong?" asked Einstein,
when Amy sat down at her desk.

Amy glanced around the room to
make sure no one was watching her.
Then she bent down and stroked the cat
while she whispered what had happened.

"That squirrel is so annoying,"
mewed Einstein. "But you can't give up
now. Do you think David will give us
another chance?"

"I don't know," said Amy. Then she sat up quickly because Mrs Damson was walking towards her with a worried-looking David by her side.

"I'm very disappointed with your results," said Mrs Damson when she looked at Amy's clipboard. "I don't understand why you didn't spot lots of wildlife in the tree. Everyone else found plenty of interesting things, and you're usually good with anything to do with animals, Amy."

"Maybe it was too noisy," said David, glowering at Nathan, who was standing just behind their teacher.

Nathan stuck out his tongue in response. "Maybe everything hid from you because they know it's your dad

who's going to cut down their tree."

David's ears went red with embarrassment. "I've already told you that's not my fault."

"And it's a ridiculous suggestion," said Mrs Damson. "Animals and birds don't think like people."

"Oh, yes we do," whispered Einstein as he rubbed himself against Amy's legs.

The class spent the rest of the lesson drawing bar charts to show everything they'd found in Home Meadow. Amy and David finished theirs very quickly because they only had one thing to put on it.

"It looks silly," said Amy. "It's going

to be the worst in the whole class."

David ran his fingers through his hair and sighed. "My first day's a complete disaster. I've messed up this project, and everyone hates me because of Dad and the tree."

"I don't hate you," said Amy. "And it wasn't just you who messed up the project. I did as well, and the squirrel didn't help."

"I know," said David. "And it's great that you're being so kind. But I wish I could go back in time and have a second chance at this project."

"Maybe we could," said Amy, as a glimmer of an idea started to form in her brain.

David stared at her in disbelief. "You

know how to travel in time?"

"Of course not. But we could still do our project again."

"Mrs Damson's not going to let us go back to the tree now," said David, shaking his head doubtfully. "She says it's maths next."

"We don't have to do it immediately." Amy's idea was rapidly developing into a proper plan. But it would only work if she could persuade David to co-operate. "We could go back to the tree after school," she suggested with an extra-friendly smile. "Late afternoon would be good – lots of animals and birds are active at that time of day."

"Are you sure we'll see more than just

a squirrel next time?" asked David.

"I'm positive," said Amy. Then she summoned all her courage and put the next step of her plan into action. "Why don't you bring your dad with you? If he sees how many creatures live in the tree, he might change his mind about cutting it down. And if he does, no one will have any reason to be cross with you any more."

David grinned. "That would be brilliant! How about I meet you at the tree at half past five. That will give me two hours to talk Dad into coming with me."

"Great," said Amy. Two hours wasn't long to put the rest of her plan into action. She'd have to hurry.

CHAPTER 5

As soon as school was finished, Amy rushed back to the Primrose Tea Room. "Come on," she said to Hilton and Plato. "We've got to get to Home Meadow as quickly as we can."

"Shall I fetch the rest of the clan?" asked the terrier.

"There isn't time," said Amy. "We'll have to manage by ourselves." Then she started to run with Hilton bounding beside her and Plato flying overhead.

It was uphill all the way to the oak tree, and Amy was puffing hard by the time they reached it. Even Hilton was panting, but Plato wasn't tired at all.

"What's that?" asked Hilton as he sniffed two flat pieces of metal lying in the grass near the base of the tree.

"They're warning signs," said Amy. "They say *Men at work*."

"I can't see any men," said Plato.

"That's because there aren't any," said Casper from a nearby branch.

Amy immediately put her hands over her head to protect herself. Then she relaxed when she saw that the squirrel wasn't holding any acorns. "So what are the signs for?" she asked. "They weren't here this morning."

"The men brought them after you left. I heard them saying they're going to cut the tree down tomorrow."

A green woodpecker popped his head out of a hole in the tree and said, "I heard them too."

"So did I," said another voice. At first, Amy couldn't see who it belonged to. Then she spotted a tiny brown wren sitting amongst the leaves. The wren spread his wings and flew down to land on her finger. "If they cut down the tree, our nest will go with it and our babies will have nowhere to live."

"Neither will mine," said the woodpecker.

Amy's stomach knotted with nerves. Everyone was depending on her, and there was so little time left. Today was her last chance to save the tree.

"What are we going to do?" asked the wren, fluttering his wings anxiously.

"That's a very good question," said Plato. He stared at Amy with his head tilted to one side. "Do you have a plan?"

"Of course I do," said Amy, with more confidence than she felt. "But I'm going to need everyone who lives in the tree to help me, and it would be easier to explain it to all of you at once."

Casper bounded up the trunk to deliver the message. Soon the tree was full of rustling and whispering and twittering. Then faces started to appear amongst

the leaves as their owners checked
to see if it was safe to come out. The
branches became
crowded with a
wide variety
of birds and
several other
squirrels as
well as Casper.
Amy could hardly
believe how many different creatures
had made the oak tree their home.
There was even a line of long-eared
bats hanging upside down as they held
onto their branch with their feet.

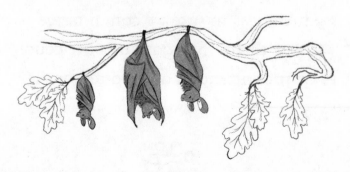

Eventually the green woodpecker said, "I think that's everyone."

"Except the insects, of course," said a rather sleepy barn owl. "They send their apologies, but they think they are a bit too small and a bit too easily eaten to get involved."

"That's okay," said Amy. "I'm sure we can manage without them." She gave a polite cough to attract attention and waited until the whispering and twittering died away. Then she quickly explained about David and his dad coming to look at the tree later that afternoon. "If Mr Townsend sees all of you, he might be so impressed that he'll change his mind about cutting down the tree."

"Are we going to sit here like this for him?" asked the woodpecker.

"No," said Amy. "That wouldn't look very natural, and it might not be interesting enough. I think it would be better if you put on a show by coming out at different times and doing different things."

"A show! I love shows," shrieked Plato, jumping up and down and flapping his wings in excitement.

"Can I be in it? Can I? Can I?"

"Don't be silly," barked Hilton. "If you were in it, the whole thing would look fake. Everyone knows parrots don't live in oak trees."

Plato sighed with disappointment. "You're right. Maybe I should go home."

"No," said Amy. "I'll need both of you to help with the show. I won't be able to talk to the birds and animals during the performance because David and his dad will hear me. So I'll be relying on you to do that for me."

Plato cheered up instantly and puffed out his chest to make him look important. Even Hilton looked pleased.

"I can help too," shouted Casper,

who was so excited that he turned a
somersault on the way down from
his branch. "I can tell everyone what
they've got to do."

"No!" shouted all the residents of the
tree together.

Casper looked surprised. "But I'd be good at that. Everyone likes me."

"No, we don't," shouted all the birds and animals again, although the result was a bit muddled because they didn't all start at the same time.

"You're too annoying," said the woodpecker.

"You say rude things about everyone," said the owl. "You told me that my eyes are too big."

"And you told me that I look as if I've had an accident with some red paint," said a plump robin with a bright red chest.

"That's not even original," said Plato. "You said nearly the same to me."

Casper shrugged. "I only do it to be funny."

"But it's not funny," said Amy. "It's horrid."

Casper stared at the ground for a moment, looking very subdued. Then he cheered up and said, "They're only pretending. They must like me really. That's why they picked me to go to talk to the clan."

The owl hooted with laughter. "We sent you so that we could have some peace and quiet while you were away. You are a very irritating squirrel."

There was a murmur of agreement from all the other residents and from Plato.

Casper looked from face to face.

Then he raised his front paws towards the other squirrels and said, "Surely *you* like me."

The other squirrels shook their heads. "You're giving us a bad name," said the largest one. "We all get the blame when you throw acorns."

Casper looked utterly miserable. His head hung low, his bushy tail drooped down to the ground and even the tufts on his ears looked less perky than they usually did. "I'm sorry," he said in a quiet voice. "Is there anything I can do to put things right?"

CHAPTER 6

Casper looked so unhappy that Amy felt sorry for him. "You need to change," she said. "Stop being rude, stop being a show-off and start being kind. Then people might start to like you."

"That's going to be so hard," wailed Casper. "But I promise I'll try." He crept sadly away and sat very still in

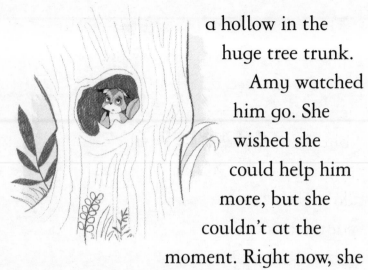 a hollow in the huge tree trunk.

Amy watched him go. She wished she could help him more, but she couldn't at the moment. Right now, she had to concentrate on making the show as good as it could possibly be. So she pulled some paper and a pencil from her pocket and turned her attention back to the other residents of the oak. "When you've all decided what you're going to do, Hilton, Plato and I will work out the order you're going to do it in."

There was a long pause filled with whispering and twittering while everyone chatted about their ideas. Eventually a bird with a blueish-grey back said, "Shall I do this?" He scurried head first down the trunk of the tree. Then he turned round and scurried back up again. "Us nuthatches are very good at running down trees like that," he announced proudly. "I'm sure it will impress David's dad."

"I'm sure you're right," said the owl. "Do you think I should do this?" He swivelled his head so far in one direction that Amy thought he was going to turn it in a complete circle. But he didn't. He stopped when his head was three-quarters of the way round and then turned it back the opposite way until he was looking forward again.

"That is very impressive," said Hilton.

Plato didn't say anything. He was too busy discovering that his own head wouldn't turn nearly as far.

"You could do that swooping-silently-down-from-the-sky thing too," suggested one of the mice who lived in a hole at the bottom of the tree. "That always scares us."

"Are you sure it won't scare David's dad?" asked another mouse.

"I'm sure it won't," said Amy. "I'll add it to the list."

There was a long pause. Then the wren wailed, "I can't do anything special."

"Neither can I," said the robin. "Does that mean we can't be in the show?"

"Of course it doesn't," said Amy. "You can both sing, and you can both fly. That's quite good enough."

"I've been thinking about the flying thing," said the leader of the long-eared bats as he stretched out his long, leathery wings. "I remember once seeing some noisy red aeroplanes give a display over the Island. They did some very impressive flying. Perhaps we could do something like that."

"By *we*, do you mean you and the other bats?" asked Hilton.

"I think we could include the birds as well. It might help those who aren't sure what to do."

"That's a great idea," said Amy. It felt strange talking to someone who was upside down, but she was still pleased that he'd volunteered to help. She raised her voice so everyone could

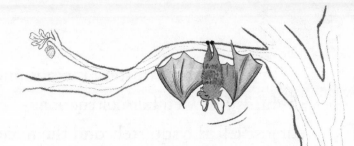

hear. "If you have wings, please talk to…" She paused as she realized she didn't know the bat's name.

"Alexander," he said.

Amy started again. "If you have wings, please talk to Alexander. He's organizing the flying display."

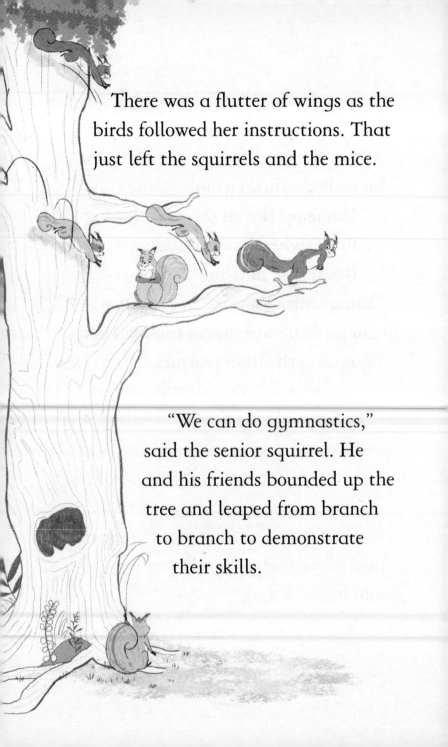

There was a flutter of wings as the birds followed her instructions. That just left the squirrels and the mice.

"We can do gymnastics," said the senior squirrel. He and his friends bounded up the tree and leaped from branch to branch to demonstrate their skills.

Amy clapped her hands in delight. "That is excellent," she said.

"Can I join in?" asked Casper from his spot beside the trunk.

"No," said the other squirrels.

"But I'm best at gymnastics."

"No, you're not," the others said. "You just think you are."

"And that's showing off," said Amy. "Remember what I said. You've got to stop being rude, stop showing off and start being kind."

"I haven't said anything nasty for at least ten minutes, and I promise that's the last showing off I'm going to do."

Just then the smallest mouse spoke in a very timid voice. "Do we have to join in?"

"Of course we do," said an elderly mouse with a touch of grey around his whiskers. "We all live here so we all have to do something."

"You only have to show you exist," said Amy. "You could just pop out of your hole and pop back in."

"That wouldn't be very interesting," said Casper.

Hilton gave a warning growl. "Are you being rude again?"

"No," said Casper. "I'm working on the being kind bit." He turned to the mice and smiled. "Would you like me to help you plan your performance?"

"Yes, please," squeaked the mice.

"Then come with me, and we'll have a practice." He led the group of mice under a nearby bush. But before they disappeared from view, he turned to Amy and said, "I hope that's all right."

"Of course it is," she replied, as she checked her list. "I'll put the mice right at the end of the show. They might be more confident if they watch everyone else do their bits first."

"Maybe they should be at the beginning so they can get it over and done with," said Hilton.

"It would be better to start with the owl," said Plato. "He could do his silent swoopy thing right over David's dad's head to attract his attention."

The three of them sat together for a while, working on Amy's list of all the entrances and exits. It was trickier than she had expected and involved a great deal of crossing out. But eventually they were all satisfied with the result, and Plato flew around the tree to tell everyone what they had decided.

"They're all busy practising hard," he said when he came back.

"I can see," said Hilton. The whole tree was alive with activity and full of the sound of birdsong.

Amy glanced at her watch. "Oh dear. That's taken much longer than I expected. David and his dad will be

here soon, and we haven't had time for a rehearsal."

"We'll just have to hope they can manage without one," said Hilton.

"I'm sure they'll be fine," said Plato. "They won't be too nervous as long as everything stays quiet and calm."

For a brief moment, everything did. Then the calmness was broken by shouts and laughter and the sound of running feet. There was something very noisy in Home Meadow, and it was coming their way.

CHAPTER 7

The noise sent all the residents of the oak tree scurrying for shelter. The mice ran back to their hole, the squirrels raced up into the safety of the branches and the birds and bats vanished amongst the leaves.

"Oh no," said Amy, jumping to her feet in despair. This was as bad as when Nathan had thrown the hoop

at the tree. What was
going on now?

She stomped out from
behind the tree trunk
and came face to face
with the whole of the
rest of her class.

"Oh, this is where you are," said Veronica, who was carrying a football under her arm. "I went to call for you, but you weren't at home."

"We've all come for a last play on the oak tree," said Jade.

"Do you have to do it now?" asked Amy.

"Of course we do," said Tom Beck, as he grabbed hold of the dangling rope and started to swing backwards and forwards. "They're going to cut it down tomorrow."

"And Jade and I have to be home in an hour," said Josie. "Mum made us promise."

"They can't stay here," Hilton whimpered. "They'll spoil everything."

"You've got to get rid of them," squawked Plato.

Nathan laughed. "I see you've got your silly animal friends with you again. Are they going to be your excuse for not climbing to the top of the tree?"

"We can do it together," said

Veronica. "It's our last chance, and Tom says he'll help."

"I can't," said Amy. She bit her lip nervously. Plato was right. She had to get rid of them or her plan would be ruined. Her mind raced as she tried to invent a reason why they had to go. But she failed. There was only one solution. She had to tell them the truth.

She took a deep breath and summoned all her courage. Then she said firmly, "You've got to go away. I've arranged with David to bring his dad here at half past five. We thought he might change his mind about cutting down the tree if we showed him how many birds and animals live in it."

"That's a great idea," said Tom.
"I don't see why that means we
have to go," Nathan argued, as he
pulled himself onto one of the lower
branches. Then he hung upside down
from it by his knees and
said, "We can show
David's dad how much
we like playing here."

Amy glared at him. "You'll be too noisy and scare the animals and birds away like you did this morning."

"How about we take my ball down to the other end of the field?" Veronica suggested. "Then he'll be able to see we like playing in Home Meadow, but we won't be in your way."

There was a murmur of agreement from the other children. "That sounds perfect," said Amy. She tapped her watch anxiously and added, "But you've got to go quickly. David and his dad will be here any minute."

She waited until her friends were a safe distance away. Then she turned back to the tree and announced, "It's all right. They've gone now."

A few heads poked out of the leaves to check she was telling the truth. Then they popped back in as David and his dad arrived. They both had identical curly hair and, to Amy's surprise, they were both wearing yellow hard hats — the sort that builders use.

"They were Dad's idea," said David. "I told him about the acorns this morning."

"It seemed a sensible precaution," said his dad in a serious voice. "I'm very pleased to meet you, Amy, but I'm not sure that I'm going to be much help with your project."

Amy was relieved to find that Mr Townsend wasn't bad-tempered like she'd expected. He seemed as friendly as his son. "Another pair of eyes will be really useful," she explained. "We're hoping to be able to spot lots of wildlife this time."

Then she led them over to a clear patch of ground with a good view of the tree. "I think this is the best place to watch from."

"Won't the dog and the parrot scare the wildlife away?" asked David.

"No," said Amy. "They're very well behaved. They belong to my great-aunt."

"No, we don't," said Plato, fluffing out his feathers in annoyance. "She belongs to us."

"Shush," whispered Amy so quietly that only the parrot and Hilton could hear. "Concentrate on running the show."

They all sat down on the grass and made themselves as comfortable as they could. Then Mr Townsend smiled and said, "Just listen to those birds singing. It sounds beautiful."

It didn't sound beautiful to Amy

because she could understand what
they were saying.

"I'm scared,"
said one
bird.
"So am
I," said
another.

"Do we really have to do this?"
said a third.

Amy crossed her fingers and hoped
the birds would be brave enough to do
everything they had worked out. This
was their last chance to save the tree.
If her plan went wrong, it would be lost
for ever.

CHAPTER 8

Amy crossed her fingers for luck as
Hilton gave a short, sharp bark – the
signal to start the show. Then the owl
swooped silently down over their heads
so close that his wings nearly brushed
Amy's hair.

"That made me jump," whispered
Mr Townsend.

The owl perched on a branch and

stared at them with wide, unblinking eyes. Then he hooted loudly and turned his head more than halfway round.

"Wow!" said David, as he wrote *owl* in the notebook he had balanced on his knees.

He'd only just finished when Hilton barked another signal, and the nuthatch appeared. He scurried down the trunk, did a pirouette and then scurried back up again.

"Was that a funny-coloured mouse?" asked David.

"No," said his dad. "It was a bird called a nuthatch. I haven't seen one of those for years."

Amy felt a flicker of hope. Mr Townsend obviously knew about birds. That should make him more likely to be impressed by the show.

Hilton gave a third bark, but this time nothing happened. Amy's flicker of hope vanished as a whisper of voices ran through the tree asking, "Who's next?"

Plato jumped up and down with impatience and squawked, "Where are the squirrels?"

Unfortunately he wasn't supposed to say anything right then. His job was to stay completely quiet until he had to squawk the signal for the flying display to start. Now he'd accidentally given that signal too early.

As the squirrels bounded out of their hiding places in the leaves, a formation of long-eared bats zoomed down from the top of the tree. They came out of their dive perilously close to the ground and then soared back up into the sky, almost colliding with a couple of squirrels showing off their ability to leap from branch to branch.

"Wow!" said Mr Townsend.

The tree was a mass of movement now. There seemed to be squirrels everywhere, scampering up and down the trunk and along the branches, leaping and somersaulting as they went. And the air was busy too with birds and bats flying in all directions.

David and his dad stared at it all with eyes wide open in astonishment. Amy stared too, but she was more worried than amazed. This wasn't what was supposed to happen. The show had to look natural, and it wouldn't if everyone crashed into each other.

"Did that robin just do a barrel roll?" said Mr Townsend. "And look at that chaffinch – it just flew a perfect loop."

"I'm amazed they can sing and fly at the same time," said David.

Amy was glad that they could. Shouts of "Watch out", "Keep left" and "Look behind you" were the only things keeping the show from disaster.

Eventually both the flying display and the squirrels' acrobatics came to an end. The birds and animals disappeared into the leaves and calm returned.

Then Hilton gave a tiny bark and Casper appeared from behind the tree. "You can come out. It's perfectly safe," he called as he ran over to the mousehole. One by one, the mice poked their noses out of the hole, sniffed the air and ran over to join the squirrel.

Then they trotted behind him in a line as he led them in a wiggly pattern through the dead leaves at the base of the tree and back to their hole.

When the last mouse was safely inside, Casper picked up an acorn and scampered towards Amy and the rest of the audience.

"Watch out," said David, pulling his hard hat more firmly onto his head.

His dad did the same, and, for the first time, Amy wished she had a hat too. But they needn't have worried, because Casper didn't throw the acorn. Instead, he stopped by Mr Townsend's feet, dug a hole in the ground and buried it carefully. Then he sat up on his hindlegs and asked, "Did I do everything right this time?"

"Definitely," barked Hilton.

"A perfect finale," squawked Plato.

"Well done," called the other squirrels from high in the branches.

Amy couldn't speak to him in front of David and his dad. But she smiled and gave a very slight nod of her head.

"That was the most amazing thing I have ever seen," said Mr Townsend, as Casper scampered happily back to the tree. "I had no idea so many creatures lived in this old oak."

"I've written them all down,"
said David, waving his notebook.
"Our bar chart will be one of the
best in the class when we redraw it."

Amy spotted her chance. "It's
a pity none of them will have
anywhere to live after the tree is cut
down."

Mr Townsend paused thoughtfully.
He looked at the *Men at work* signs
lying on the ground. Then he looked
up at the tree, where dozens of small
faces looked back at him from
between the leaves. The birdsong
was different now. It was saying,
"Please, please, please," but he
didn't know that.

Eventually, he looked at David and Amy and said, "I think we should keep this old oak after all. Animals and birds are more important than a pretty view, aren't they?"

Amy grinned. "The view will be pretty anyway with such a beautiful tree in it."

Then she and David ran out onto the field, waving their hands and shouting, "The tree is safe!"

The rest of the juniors raced across the grass to the tree, shouting with delight.

"Thanks for changing your mind," Veronica said to Mr Townsend.

"And for letting us use Home Meadow," said Tom Beck.

"Do you want to play football with us, David?" said Nathan.

"Yes please," said David as he ran to join his new-found friends.

Only Amy heard the voices of the squirrels in the oak tree above them. "Do you want to play with us?" said one of them.

"Yes please," said Casper. "And I promise not to be annoying any more."

AMY'S WILDLIFE SPOTTER'S GUIDE

Find out more about some of the creatures who live in Casper's tree

Red squirrel

In the UK, the red squirrel is only found in a few places and never in the same area as the more common grey squirrel. Has ear tufts, unlike its grey cousin. Seen mostly in woods. Eats seeds of cones, buds, berries, bark and nuts.

Brown long-eared bat

Seen at dusk. Catches flying insects and flies in a jerky fashion. Sleeps in hollow trees or dark buildings during the day.

Woodmouse

Active at night. Good climber and jumper. Digs burrows. Eats buds, berries, seeds and nuts.

Robin

Brick-red breast, brown wings and back. Sings all year round, through winter and, if it's near street lights, even at night.

Green woodpecker

Pigeon-sized. Often seen on the ground, hunting ants. Green wings and back, red "cap". Call sounds like loud laugh.

Barn owl

Often nests in old buildings or hollow trees. Hunts small mammals and birds at night. Its call is an eerie shriek.

Nuthatch

Greyish-blue head and wings, golden-brown breast, very short tail, black eye stripe. Walks head first down tree trunks.

To find out more about the birds you can spot in your local park or garden, try Usborne Minis Birds to Spot

LOOK OUT FOR MORE
AMY WILD ADVENTURES...

AND THE QUARRELLING CATS

When some of Amy's cat friends
discover that their food is going missing,
poor Bun gets the blame. Amy is
determined to clear his name, so she
sets out to solve the mystery. Can she
find the real greedy thief before the cats'
quarrel ruins their friendship
for ever?